T0067118

VAMPIRE MOM

LINDA LE'MAY

authorHOUSE®

AuthorHouse™
1663 Liberty Drive
Bloomington, IN 47403
www.authorhouse.com
Phone: 1 (800) 839-8640

Published by AuthorHouse 02/12/2015

ISBN: 978-1-4969-6784-8 (sc)
ISBN: 978-1-4969-6783-1 (e)

Print information available on the last page.

This book is printed on acid-free paper.

Contents

ABOUT THE BOOK

This book is inspired by my crazy, loving, and misunderstood family, with all the love from my heart. I hope this book can make people understand the lonely heart can be a broken soul as well so, take care and take care of those that are tender hearted as well.

After Linda's sixth brithday, her mother felt it was time to tell Linda a little more about her father. So, she stuck her head out of the door way,and asked Linda to come to to her mothers bed room. Linda jumped up from the floor, and scurried to her mother room as she was asked to. When Linda entered the bed room, she noticed that her mother had a box. Linda watched, as her mother dumped the box over onto the foot of the bed. Linda asked her mother," mom what is this stuff ?" Her mother replied," Linda this is pictures, and articales of your father. That I wanted you to look at. Linda did look at some of the pictures. There were only two that took Linda's attion. One was of her father in an air force uniform. Linda thought, some one in her family that flue planes was cool. Untill her mother explained that he only worked on them ont flue them. Linda still thought even getting that close to an air plane was still cool. Then the other one showed him standing next to her Uncle Jesse, and holding a baby. Her mother then explained that the baby was indeed Linda. As Linda took a more cloesly look at the picture. She noticed how her father, and herself had the same pale complextion, and dark hair. Then Linda took the piture to a mirror to see if they even had the same eye color. To Linda's surprize they indeed did. They had the very same dark redish brown eyes. Linda then truned with great happiness, and said," mom now I know were I get my looks from, it's my dad." Her mother replied," yes, I know." Then, Linda notied a news paper clipping. It was old, and a little ripped. You could bearly make out the head line. Which read," MAN SHOT WHILE STEALING." Linda look at it, then at her mother, and asked," whats this?" Her mother explained," well, your father wasn't no saint. Your father had done things that in curiouasty. After the guys toke off doing thier thing, Linda, and her mother was off to the grave site to were Peter was burried. It seemed like for ever in getting to the graves. As they pulled up a long narrowed road, Linda was able to see the graves on ethir side of the road. When they came to the open end to were they entered the grounds. Linda was beginning to get goose bumps running up, and down her arms. Linda was beginning to feel her hart beat rappidly, as they came arround the back side. When they begun to slow down, Linda's palms were sweeting. She tried to dry them off by rubbing them in her pants leg, before she open the door to get out. Even though it didn't do much good. As, Linda made her way around the car, her mother pointed out the grave. Linda looked at her mother as if to say, will you go with me. But, her mother told her to go ahead whats is he going to do jump and getcha. with a brave face Linda just nodded her head, and proceaded alone to her fathers grave. After walking up to Peters head stone, Linda took a deep relaxing breath as she looked arround befor really looking at his stone. Linda noticed that everyone of them looked the same. They all was small white sqares in a perfect line, with american flags on each plot. As Linda looked down at Peter's headstone, Linda notied how worn the letering were. She also notied how dead the grass looked around his plot. and how the plot was mainly sand. When Linda trun to face her mother once again. She heard her name being called out in a sot wisper. Linda rose her head up to see were the sound was coming from. Thats when she saw something like a black shadow run pass her out of the corner of her eyes. Linda looked around more agressively, but she didn't see anything. Linda just dissmissed it as nothing more than her imagenation running away with her. She began to walk toward to the car, were her mother was waiting for her. When Linda got half way to her mothr she heard her name being called out once more. Linda stoped walking, and truned around to face were the sound was. First Linda closed her eyes. Then when she stoped trunnig around, she opened her eyes to she were she was faceing. In surprize Linda found her self faceing her father's grave. Linda shookher head from side to side, and said to her self," whats wrong with me? I know i've just been in this old grave yard to long now I'am hearing, and seeing things." When Linda made it to the car, she told her mother," I'am ready to go now."" O.k." replied her mother."

As they were leaveing the grave yard, Linda was paying more attion to the head stones. On the way out of the drive, Linda could bearly see her father's creepy grave. She seen to her surprize the shadow that ran by her. It just stood there, As if to say i'll be seeing ya later. Linda, quikly asked her mother," why was Peter's grave looks so unkept?"" I don't know ", answered her mother. Linda looked out the window once more to see if they passed the graves yet. When see started to see houses, Linda knew see could relaxs.

When Linda and her mother made it home, they got out of the car, and went inside to get ready for the guys to get home. After the guys got home the wemen had supper ready to be consumed. As the guys sat down to eat, Linda, and her mother would make fun of how they were eating. When supper was over Linda, and her mother cleaned up the kitchen. After the kitchen was cleaned, the wemen went to the living room to watch t.v. with the guys. Not long after a few shows went off, Linda's dad told everyone to go to bed for the night.

After a year gone by, and money problems arised. The family decided to move to Linda's grandmothers house. Then one moring Linda's dad started to go out to look for work. Instead mother nature decieded to rain. Then he just turned back around and said to his self," forget this I ain't going out and get my self killed. over sum dumb window wipers. He reached up to hang his keys back up. After he fixed himself a cup of coffee. Then sat at the kitchen table to wait out the rain. By that time, the other family membrs has all riasen from bed, and with it being Saturday. The kids ehought they could run out side to play. Instead thier father stoped them in there tracks, and said," ya'll can't go out side right now it's rainin."

The kids then decided to trun to the kitchen to only find thier grandmother standing over the coffee pot. Then they came running over to were she was, and asked if she could tell more stories." Happy to", replied thier grandmother. As several stories went by, Linda's dad noticed the rain began to stop. He reached to the hanger by the door and said," we'll it stop rainin now. I'am come to look for work." Linda's mom replied," ok dear, be caerful and good luck," as he went out to the truck. The boys wanted to go out side to play in the mud. Thier mother said to them to go get out have fun. But Linda wanted to hear more stories, but this time about her father Peter. Her grandmother thought for a minute, and said," sure I think I know a few." With excitement Linda ran beside her mother, to face her grandmother. So, she could hear her better.

As her grandmother began to tell her stories, Linda began to hear wispers. They wasn't loud enough to drown out what was being said so, Linda deicieded to ingnore it. It worked for a while, but through the fith story the wisper got louder, this time Linda can make out what was being said,. Linda looked up at her mother slowly to see if she heared the same thing. Her mother just looked back at Linda and smiled. Linda knew that she was the only one that could hear this going on, because her grandmother was still talking. At this time this voice was no longer a wisper, but a voice calling out to her. Linda was beginning to fell uneasy, as this voice kept calling to her....Linda, Linda, Linda,Linda. At that moment Linda happened to looked down toward the middle fo the floor. There it grew, a deep dark blak hole was forming. Linda once again looked at her mother as to say help me. But, once again her mother just smiled at her. Knowing that this thing was only targgering at Linda, Linda grew more afarid. Then all the sudden out of nowere, Linda jumped down to the floor and ran around the as if to tippy toe around it. She jumped up beside her grandmother,and took a big bite out of her arm. As blood came trickleing down the side of her grandmothers arm, and her grandmother hollering out in pain,and surprizement of whats happening. Linda's mother inshock came running to her rescue. As Linda's mom was pounding down on her head, Linda could hear the voice laughing at her. When Linda let lose her grandmother's arm, she noticed the black hole was gone, and the voice stopped. After all this, her mother told her to go to her bed room untill she could tell them, why in the world would make her do what she did. Linda didn't know why. All she knew was she felt compeld to do so, and she didn' t know what to tell them. After a while Linda's be late." I know, we just like it better this way. Its more like a game this way." Remarked Linda. Bill would hurry to his class, as Linda would prepare for hers. For two years things seemed pretty cool. Linda, and Bill went to school, and home with no troubles, and this was the year that James started preschool too. But, not at the same school.

One day, Linda has been feeling ill. She didn't want to tell any one, Because she didn't want to miss school. Linda want to be in school more than home any way. It wasn't because she was a nerd or any thing. She was just tired of listening to her parenets argue. After the same rutine every morning, Linda began to fell sick. Than again she heard a voice. Linda sort of looked around to see if any one was picking at her. But, there was no one. Linda tried to ignore the voice. She couldn't, it just grew louder in her ears. Linda wispered what do you want. In a kind and gentle voice, it said," Billy Joe". Linda was confussed," What?," she asked. The voice said again in a calm voice, "death." Linda was scared. She didn't know what was going on. All she knew to do was to cry. When the teacher asked Linda what was wrong. Linda wouldn't answer. She just sat there. The teacher just got anoid, adnd sent her to the counsler to see what was wrong. Then agian Linda didn't say a thing. The counsler decieded to let Linda just rest on the couch for a while, and then send her back ot her class room. After awhile Linda did feel better and wanted to go back to class all by her self.

After school was out Linda had a sick feeling falling all over her. Linda didn't want to say any thing to Bill. She thought he'll just make fun of her again, like he all ways did when she has a feeling about something. Just to pass the time, and to put these thoughts out of her head. Linda, and Bill would throw rocks into the conale as they walked home. If not that, they would do the signal to get the big simmi trucks to blow there horns. After a while Linda, and Bill would trun down Still Will street, and the distance Linda could see the mail box to the drive way. Seeing this that feeling came rushing back as warning that something isn't right. When the two kids made thier way up the drive way, to the camper. When they entered, they saw their parents seated at the table cring. Bill asked," whats wrong?" Whats going on?" They truned to Bill, and said, "Billy Joe drowned in the pond to day, and the er came, and took him away. Linda, and Bill started to cry. Linda said to her self," I knew it." After a week, they had the funeral, it was small but nice. The grave yard was just as small. It had a horse shoe drive way, and a small square white building. Later Linda's parents placed a double hearted head stone, with a palm tree planted behind it.

About six months later Linda's mother had another baby. His name is Bobby Ray Malphrus. He was a cute little blonde headed boy, with blue eyes. Then some time later, Linda's family moved to Sun Coast were James started kindergarden. Not long after being there Linda met a friend that told her about church and had asked if she wanted to go. Linda didn't know to much about church, but wanted to try it.

After awhile Linda has grown to love church. At first Linda didn't know what to think, but she thought she would keep an open mind. The more Linda whent to church, the more she wanted her family to go. After awhile Linda's brothers started to go to church, and they also wanted thier mother to go too. For a long time thier mother didn't want to go to church. But, after awhile she caved in, and decided to go. Linda was really pleased. they all went to church on every Sunday, Sunday nights, and Wednesday night. They all were very happy. Then One day Linda just felt an urge to go to the front alter. As Linda aproched it, she fell onto her legs. There faceing down on the steeple, Linda found her self crying her eyes out. By the time she was done crying, Linda heared her self begging for forgiveness. This was strange for her because, she nevered asked or even begged to be forgived or even apolagized for anything. By the time Linda was able to lift her legs up off the floor, to her surprize she found her brothers, and her mother doing the same thing. Not long after Linda, her mother, and her brothers all got baptized. For doing so Linda didn't hear anymore voices, or haveing anymore viziones.

Maybe not long after, another baby was born with a defect. which Linda some how all ready knew about, named Joseph. Her mother told everyone that Joseph would be going back to the hospital to correct the split in his lip. Then he'll be normal again. Linda wispered under her breath," normal is under rated. But, in time Linda learned to love all her little brothers.

Things when't well for a while, no voices, no vizions that no one could hear or see in that matter. Then, one night, Linda bolted up in bed, very scared, and up set crying. She slowly walked out of her bed room. As she made her way throught the hallway, and kitchen, she noticed her dad sitting in his lay back chair. With tears running down her face, she made her way to him. As her dad looked up from his paper, and saw Linda standing there sobbing, he asked her," whats worng ?" Linda began to tell him about her dream. With that he reached out to confort her in his lap trying to tell her how he isn't going any were fast. That he will allway be there for her. Linda was conviced that her dream ment some thing, and she was trying to tell him how the ground just opened up and swallowed him up, and how it happened to them one by one. Her father didn't lisen to her warning, He just brushed off as a night mare. All he could do was just rock Linda back and forth in his chair till she was calm enough to go back to sleep. As Linda started to drift off to sleep Linda heard DADDY'S HANDS playing on the radio. By the time the song was over, her daddy toted her to bed. Were Linda slept the rest of the night.

A few weeks gone by,and Linda's mother decided to take the kids swimmin at the beach with her sister, and her three kids. While everyone was swimming, Linda decided to stay under the big umbrella. She didn't fell like being in all that sun. Linda was beginning to fell a little sick to her stomake, so, she tried to barry part of her legs in the sandy beach. It worked to her surprize. After awhile Linda Started to fiddle around with the ring on her finger. She began to twist it around, and around untill it fell off her finger in to the sun light. As soon Linda went to reach for it, she got seriously burned. As quickly as posible Linda pulled back her hand. Linda started to panic, untill she reallized that her feet were still sticking out of the shade. But they were under the cool sand. Then she had an idea. She shoved her arm under the sand, as far as she could go under the ring. Then she made a worlly motion in the sand untill the ring started to sink in to her hand. She quikly pulled thr ring to her, and put the ring back on the finger that it came off of. Then for a brife moment in time Linda was confuessed. After putting the ring back on, she put her hand back out in the sun, and to her surprize... her hand didn't go up in bubbleling burns. When Linda was going to see once more what would happen if she would take off the ring again, her mother walked up and said," Linda go wash off in the water so, we could go home now. We are getting ready to go now ok." Linda shoved the ring back in place, and said," yes mame."

A few moments later, after making it to the car, Linda's mother realized that the car keys were still locked up in the trunk of the car. Befor she started to panic, Her sister told an idea she had to retrive the keys. Linda's mother agreed with her sister, and started to go through the back seat, With disapoint ment they saw that they were to big to fit throw trhe space. Yet, after looking very closely at the space, Linda's mother asked her sister," Debby couldn't Kathy fit through the space?" "Oh yea," as Debby replied, she truned to her daughter. Kathy come here and see if you could fit through this small space. So, you could reach the keys in the back." "Yes mame," answered Kathy. After climbing in the space Kathy called out," it's to dark I can't see anything. I need some kinda light, so, I could see something." A second later her mother handed her a small flash light. Kathy thanked her mother and trun on the flash light. She spotted the keys, She tried to reach for them. As she reached for the keys, she said out loud," all most...allll moosstt. "Then In just instant she shouted," got it!" As she backed her self out, every one saw how sweaty she was. Every one got into the car and went home.

After getting home, the phone rang. Linda was beginning to feel nrevous. She didn't understand why, untill she heard her mother on the phone. When ever her mother got off the phone, she annouced that it was the doctor, and that Bill has gotten hurt and for her to come to the hospital. Then she asked," Debbie do you mind staying here and look after the kids for me?" "Sure sis, do what ever you have to do. I'll be right here." answered Debbie.

As thier mother left, Linda, and her brothers watched her drive off. Bill asked," I wondered what happened?" James said," I know, He shot him self in the foot with the nail gun." No, wait, I know he fell in the cement tub and got dried, like on Right Turn Clyde." As they sort of snickered about it, Debbie snucked up on them, and told them cut it out, as Linda wispered under her breath," I really know what happened to him. I bet he fell from a very high place. Not listening to what thier Aunt Debbie saying, the boys were running a muck. Linda got tired of the yelling the boys were doing, so Linda decided to yell above her Aunt Debbie and said," will you guys shut up all ready and do as she says. Now go take what ever showers she said to take and go to bed all ready." Debbie looked at Linda in great surprize and told her how thankful she was with her help. Linda replied," don't worry about it. I just have an headake and I am ready for bed too." Ok, Linda go ahead and I'll wait for your mother to get back. When your brothers are done, I'll send them to bed to after they eat of course.

Chapter 3
WHAT TO DO

Late that night Linda's mother came home, and her mother's sister abid them good bye, and went home her self. After watching the head lights leave, Linda's mother entered Linda's bed room to wake her up. As she was getting Linda up for a moment, she told Linda," I need you to get your brothers up in the morning for school for me just in case iam not here to do it ok." Bearly awake Linda answers," yes mame I will.

That morning came, and at no surprize Linda's parents wern't home. So, Linda did as she promised she would do. Linda got Bill, and James up for school. After sending them off to school, Linda stayed home with Bobbt Ray, and Joseph. They were just to young to understand whats going on. Linda didn't say much excipt for go clean your room, or if there is more food in there less room to be talking. Linda didn't feel right to answer any of their questions as they would put it. After feeding her little brothers, Linda tried to clean up the house a little bit untill thier mother got home.

Later that evening, Linda's mother came home from the hospital. She told Linda," don't worrie your father will be home in a few days, and untill then your two younger brothers will be with your Aunt Debbie's house. So, when you get your brothers up for school, you con go too, understand."" Yes mame," answered Linda. "Good, now I am going to take a shower and run back up to the hospital to make sure your daddy won't need anything or even the doctors in that madder." replied Linda's mother. Right before she left, Linda asked her mother what to feed her brothers in case they get hungery. Linda's mother replied, I don't know just find them sumethin, I got to go. Just don't use the stove." "O.k. mom I will." responded Linda in a hurry out the door to follow her mom to the car. As her mother drove off, she gave Linda a small smile of incoragement.

After a couple of hours later, Linda's brothers came home looking around. When they saw Bobby Ray, and Joseph, they trun to Linda asking," were is mom? Is mom still with dad at the hospital? When is mom coming home?" All Linda could say is I don't know. When Bill, and James got tired of the same answers to thier quistion, they just went to thier room to play the intendo. Linda figured she would have at lest a few hours befor they start holloring for food. But, she was wrong, it only took 30 minutes. Linda looked every were for some thing to feed them. Just then, she found the family size of raviolys to feed every one. All the boys were happy once again. After they all ate, Linda then put all the boys to bed. Linda streached her arms out, and told them that she'll be right in the living room, if they need her.

After several hours, Linda's mother came in the trailer with a look of happiness on her face. Linda asked her, "Whats up mom?" Teresa replied," your father will be coming home in the morning." While hearing such great news, Linda jumped to her feet, and gave her mother a big hug. When the excitement settled down, Linda, and her mother spent another hour watching the t.v. set, and eatting whats left of the raviolys, before going to bed.

That morning came, and Linda was the first up. She has gotten breackfast done. After letting Bill, and James eat, she sent them off to school. Then she went to her mothers door to wake her up. Linda told her mother that she was gonna get ready for school too. Her mother barely spoke through the door and said, "hold up Linda, I'll take you to school on my way to the hospital." Linda replied, "o.k."

30 minutes later, Linda, and her mother got Bobby, and Joseph up, and dressed. After the two boys got done eatting, they all loaded up in the mini van. After dropping Linda off at school, Teresa started off to the Hospital.

At arrival, Teresa parked at the parking area at the back of the hospital. When Teresa went to the front desk, she asked for the room for Bill Malphrus. After the woman told Teresa, she went on to Bills room. As she entered his room, Teresa notice Bill's doctors reading his chart. Teresa asks," whats the vredic doc." The doctor replied," you must be his wife." Teresa nods her head. The doctor continues," well it's like this...your husband has cancer." With the look of shoock on her face, Teresa replies," what do you mean he has cancer. Were do you get from falling from a building to cancer?" The doctor responded intent to calming her down," Mrs. Malphrus your husband had cancer for a very long time. Infact untill now it has been asleep. It's just woke up when he hit his leg on the rafters on the way down. But for now he needs bed rest and a couple of days of supervion, and then he'll be able to go home."

Meanwhile at school, around lunchbreak Linda was feeling a little alone and depressed. Linda was begining to fight with her emotions. As she was struggling with her self she was begining to her taughting voices again. Not like the usaul ones that she would normally would her from other students at school. Linda tries to ecnor them as if it didn't happen. As the bell rung Linda got up to get in line for the last piorde of the day. When the day ended, Linda was happy to go home. As Linda cault up with Bill, she suggested that they would take the woods home. With a smile Bill said." o.k. but lets wait for Penny and Gersiom." Linda replied with a smile, "o.k."

When ever Penny, and Gershiom found Linda, and Bill, Bill filled them in on the plan to going home. They agreed, and suggested going by the coveret. They knew that it still would be full of water, and more likely go in the water to cool them selfs off. While slideing down the coverets and hitting the deep in, Linda hit an under toll. As she fights her way to the top, Linda felt Bill land right on top of her. When Bill kicked his way back to the top, he wind up busting Linda in the nose. With a little blood coming out, they all agreed that it was time to go home.

As Bill and Linda snuck back into the trailer, they noticd that there mother hasn't made it home yet. With little curiosty, Linda and Bill ran to thier rooms to change thier clothes. A few moments later their mother has drove up the drive way. As they watched their mother walk up to the door,they noticed thier father wasn't with thier mother. When she entered the living room, she noticed Linda and Bill was stareing at her as if in waiting for an commit of some kind. With that thier mother just replied." ya'lls dad will be home sone ok." The kids then replied," ok." Linda. and Bill darted off to play Bill's intendo.

A couple days latter,Teresa, and Linda, and the four boys whent to the hospital to pick up thier father, after the doctor called the house. As they entered the hopital parking lot, Linda, and her brothers noticed how huge the hospital was. As the got out of the car, Linda noticed how clean every thing was. When they entered the main office, Teresa asked the nurse if Bill Malphrus was still in the same room. The nurse replies," one moment please. Ok, Bill Malphrus right?" Teresa answered," yes." The nurse continued," ah, yes he is in the same room." Teresa replies, thank you, as she started off to the elavator with kids following after her.

As Teresa, and the kids entered Bill's room, they just cault the middle of the story of how Bill wind up in the hospital. As Bill continued," But the foreman wouldn't stop hounding me on my lunch break. So, just to shut him up, I went up to finish the work I tried to tell him I couldn't do. As I was up there doing what i do best. I heard it,The dam borad was cracking up from under neath me. When I tried to get off', it was to late i came falling down. I knew I had to do something. So, I tried reaching for anything, and when I did I whent swingging. When I did that, I hit my leg hard.

That's how my knee got swollen." Then across the room stood Aunt Susan. She asked her brother," how far did you fall again." Bill replied," Two stories." Then Uncle Bill spoke up and said, Dam Bill you could've died out there you need to be more carefull." By that time a nurse came in, and told everyone that they need to leave the room so she could clean and change Bill's bandage. As they all left the room the doctor came in Bill's room and said," I have bad news and good news. Which do you want first?" Bill looked up at the doctor from his sponge bath and replied," doc give me the bad news first." With a sad look on his face he told Bill that he has cancer setting up in his leg and they may need to capatate his leg. In fustration Bill asked," what about work? How ami supposed to take care of my family? Construction is all I know. Doc what will happen if I keep my leg?" As the nurse finishes up with the bandages around Bill's leg, the doctor replies," will Mr. Malphrus you will have at least 6 months without cemo treatment and a year with cemo treatment. Then you just mite die you might last a little longer I don't know. All I do know is that this cancer is a killer." Bill asks the doctor," how long do i have to make a decession?" The doctor replied," Befor you leave here and tha was the good news you can leave today." I have to talk with my family first please," answered Bill. As the doctor left the room he told Bill's family that they may reenter the room now.

As the family enter the room, they noticed a warey look on his face. Teresa asked Bill," whats the matter hun?" Bill told them the hole story and waited for a responds. Aunt

Susan asked," bub aren't you gonna take the surgery?" Irratated Bill answered," wasn't you listening to what I said. dam sis your hard headed." Teresa told everyone to leave and let them talk it over.

Teresa told Bill that she loves him and will support him in what ever decession he makes. Bill replies in tears and said," baby I have to keep my legs so i can work to take care of you and the kids. You know if I did do that I would have to stay home and that will drive me insane and you know that when we stayed with Kathy and Guy for a little bit." Befor Teresa could respond the nurse came in with Bill's clothes and told him that the doctor will be in with his release papers. Then the nures left the room.

When the doctor entered the room he asked Bill," well whats your verdict?" Bill answered," doc iam keeping my leg."" I figured that you'll say that. So, I made arrangements were you could see a regular doctor for your cheak ups ok." Bill answeres," sure doc what ever you say." As the the doctor handed Bill's release papers he said," no son it's what ever you say." and truned to walk out the room.

As they all drove home Linda was listening to everything her parents were saying and linda finally let the news of her father dieing sinking in. Linda tries to hold all her tears in. When they all drove up to the trailer, they all ate supper and got ready for school the next day.

As Linda arose up from bed, Linda didn't really feel very good. She tried to tell her mother, but she didn't want to hear it. She told Linda to get dressed for school. Linda did as she was told. While walking to the buss stop with Bill Bill they talked about what was said the other day. When Linda started to talk about thier father dieing, Bill Bill tried to walk away from Linda, but Linda reminded Bill Bill that they go to the same school and there's no reason to try to get away from her. Then Linda saw Penny Parr, her best friend. Linda walked swiffly over to her as, started to talk about Penny's weekend. By that time the buss pulled up and Penny and Linda sat togther. While Bill Bill sat with Gersiom Parr, Penny's little brother.

As all the kid unloaded the buss, Linda and Penny went to breakfeast, while Bill Bill and Gershiom went to thier classes. After breakfeast Linda and Penny went thier sepreat ways and went to thier class. While in class Linda was enjoying her self, untill the fourth period, which was reading class. While Linda was reading her asigned reading book, Linda came across the word (dead). Lindda started to think about her father again. Linda was trying to hold back all emotions.

After reading class was over, it was lunch time. Linda was to emotional to eat. She just slurped around on her choclate milk. When it was gone Linda dropped off her plate. After dropping off her plate Linda slowly walked out side were you would wait for the bell to ring. Linda couldn't stop the emotions from coming out. Linda friskly walkd out toward a mettal box and sunked down. Linda started to cry. While crying Linda asked God," why him, why my daddy. Take me instead of my daddy. We need him." As Linda realizing that there wasn't going to be any answering to her questions, she saw some broken glass. In between tears Linda picked up a pice of glass and looked at it on ethier side. Just then she heared a voice once agian tauting her," DO IT, YOU KNOW THERE IS NO OTHER OPTION. DO IT, IT'S THE ONLY WAY." As Linda started to strike her wrist, a student came around the corner. When the student saw what Linda was doing, she yeald out for a teacher for help.

As the teacher came to the student's aide, the student told the teacher what she saw. The teaacher then turned to Linda, which was still sitting on the ground, and grabbed her by the arm. The teacher told Linda that she is now be going to the counselor. When they arrived at the counselors office, the teacher told Mrs. C every thing. Mrs. C the truned to Linda and asked, "is this was true?" Linda replied," yes mam." Why would you do such a thing for?," asked Mrs. C." Because. my dad is dieing and I thought if could take his place he wouldn't have to go." answered Linda. Ok Linda, but think about this. What if, this dosen't work and your dad dies anyway and there is no one to help your mother?" asked Mrs. C. Linda didn't answer. She just sat there, thinking about what Mrs. C just said. A few moments later Mrs. C told Linda," you can sit there untill you feel confortable to go back to class." Quitely Linda answeres," ok".

Linda must stayed in Mrs. C's class for at least an hour. When Linda finally went to class, it seems that every eye was on her. Like as if Linda was about to give a speach. When everyone seen that Linda wasn't going to say anything, they all truned to thier desks and continued thier work.

After school, Linda didn't say much to Bill Bill or James onthe way home. James knew something was wrong with Linda, because they were so close. they were like best friends. When James asked his big sister what was wrong, she answered," nothing is wrong ok.' Then James asked," are you ok sis." Linda then replied," i am fine now. I am with my best buba," James then smiled and replied," good.

As the buss arived at the buss stop, Linda, James, and Bill Bill got off the buss. Then they begun to walk to the trialer. As Linda entered the trailer, she had a surpize waiting for her. Linda's mother and father was waiting for her in the living room.

Chapter 5

DEPRESSION

As Linda was doing her homework in the kitchen table, her parents were watching her. When Linda pronounced that her homework was done, her parents told Linda that they wanted to talk to her. When Linda went to the living room, the four brothers came into the living room to ask, to go out side. Teresa, and Bill told the boys, sure go ahead just don't leave the yeard. Then they trun ther attion back to Linda. Her father said," I heard that you tried to kill yourself today?" Linda looked shocked and surprizesed. Linda atural to her self how did ya'll find out. Then in respeact she answered her father," yes sir," Her mother then implied," why...why would you want to do such a thing like that?" Linda started to explain, then her father aturalg and said," *you know dam well better then that. We didn't raise you to be a dam quiter like that." In aturalg Linda's father walked out of the trailer, and started to work on his ford truck.*

In a calm voice, Linda's mother explained," there is never a good reason to kill your self. What if your brothers found out? How do you think they would react to this? What about your future? Don't you want to graduate? How would you be able to join the army if your all ready dead? I mean don't you want kids one day?" All these questions hit Linda. She wasn't sure how to answer them. Then out the blue, Teresa told Linda that Mrs. C. told them what happen that day. All Linda could say in atural," oh."

Later that night, after everyone got cleaned up, and ate supper. The family retired into the living room, and watched a movie atural. After the movie, everyone gave them selves a big streach and headed for bed. Early that morning Linda got up for school, but she didn't realized how early it was.

As Linda entered the kitchen, her father just got done atura breakfast. Bill saw Linda standing there in the entrance way rubbing her eyes, and asked," why are you up so early. Do you know it's only 15 to 5:00 in the morning?" Linda just shook her head as she atural her shoulders." Well I am glad your up cause I wanted to talk to you any way. Come here and set next to me here" asked Bill. Now Linda, tell me why did you try to do what you I to do yesterday" asked Bill. Linda slowly said," because I thought you were gonna die. So I was gonna try to keep you here cause I love you daddy." Bill replied," Linda I am not going anywere fast. Besides, no one knows when anyone is going to die or not, and Iam not going anywhere. I love you too Linda, but you got to stop this crap right now, understand?" Linda replied," yes sir, I understand." Now go back to bed atur it's time for you to get ready for school ok." Explained Bill." Yes sir," answered Linda."

Later that morning Linda got back up out of bed, and got ready for school. First Linda got breackfast going, that way she didn't have to eat breakfast at school. Eventhough she knew that she would any way. After atura Linda told Bill Bill, and James that they only have so many minutes to get ready, and eat. By that time Penny and Gerishom came over to remind Linda and her brothers about the buss. Bill Bill, and James just grabed their pancakes off the table,and rolled it up like a tube. As they started to eat it on the way to the buss stop, Linda quikly cleared the table, and ran behind them to the buss stop.

While at school things ran as there normal rate. Linda can't stand the students and the students couldn't stand her. Linda atura thought once she passed the fith grade to the sixth grade things should be better. That was her new focuse. This was what Linda wanted to think about. She didn't want to think about anything els.

After school Linda, and her brothers took I time going home they didn't want to face home. Of course there it was. As Linda walked into the door, she saw her mother picking up the phone. Linda's brother were pushing there way in the door. After atural up the phone, Teresa started to trun to face Bill, but noticed the worried look on her daughter's face." Come and sit next to your father, Linda, "asked Teresa. Linda did what her mother asked. Then Linda's mother continued," it was the doctor on the phone. He wants your father and I go to the doctors office for some treatments. He said that the appointment was for tomarrow at 10 am." Bill replies," ok then I gusse well talk tomarrow night." Linda looked at her parents with atura and asked," can I go out side now." Her father looked at his watch ao his wrist and said," yes, for a little while then you and your brothers would have to come in," With a smile on Linda's face she ran out the door to breath in the fresh air.

That night Teresa stuck her head out the door to tell the kids to come in and get cleaned up for supper. After supper Bill tell the kids to take a bath and get ready for bed for school tomarrow. When it was Linda's trun to take a bath, she would clean out the tub enough to were it is decent. Then she would set the cold and warm water were it would be luke warm. After setting the water, Linda would slowly take off her clothes to were she could get used to the climent in the room. Then she would climb into the tub, and shut the shower atural. After that Linda would slip down into the tub, and atural her self under the water to were only her face is above the water. Then she would relax atur the water is filled. By the time Linda got out of the tub, it was supper time. After atura, they all got ready for bed, because I father was to tired to watch a movie that night.

The atural day was just like any other day. Getting out of bed, doing mornig chore, helping her brothers get ready for school. At school everything was about the same also, kids picking on Linda, calling her names. Linda just ignoreing them as usual. Then Mrs. C called Linda to the office. Linda went to see what she wanted. Linda entered Mrs. C office and sat down into a chair in front of Mrs. C desk. Mrs. C looked up from her desk, to see if Linda was sitting confortablely. Mrs. C asked," so, have you spoke to your parents?" Linda looked at Mrs. C. with atural and anger, and said," yes I did. Why did you tell them for?

Don't you know you weren't supposed to add stress to my father. Besides that I thought this was conferdental." Then Linda said to her self you dum bitch. Mrs. C then add," Linda it was a life or death concern. I am bound to my duty to tell your parents." Linda then thought to her self, Yea right I bet. Then in a sarcastic voice," You've made my day. I'll never trust another cousler again for as long as I live. May, I go now?" Mrs. C then answered," yes you may." Linda then spent the rest of the school day up set.

When the day was done, Linda, and her two brothers got off the the buss. Linda just realized that her mother and father had to go to the doctor's offfice that day. When Linda entered the living room, Linda saw how sad they were, she had to ask," whats the matter. Teresa replied," the doctor told us that the cancer has progressed and there isn't much they can do but cemo and medication." Linda didn't know what to say to the news she just recived, Linda just went to her room with tears in her eyes, and stayed there for the rest of the night.

Wasn't long Linda begun to have an attude with everyone, even people at the church. Linda just didn't know how to express he anger and aturalg. If people asked her what was wrong, and she would try to explain. People would just start to think that she was nuts. So, she figured that she would rather try to take each day, one day at a time.

While Linda is trying to find her self again, she kept going to church just because her mother asked her. Which ment that her brothers continued to go also. After awhile their father decieded to go to church, and after a week he also got saved in the process. When Linda saw her father get saved, her out look begun to change once again.

Couple days later while the kids were in school but Bobby and Joseph, Teresa had to rush Bill back to the hospital. When they got to the hospital, the doctor said to Teresa and Bill," I am going to keep you here for awhile to see if there is any change." Bill say's," for how long?" The doctor replied," it would be about a week. At least then we will know if this medication would work better. This way you woun't be in here for awhile, hopefully a long while."" Ok, but, what about work? You know money to keep food in tummys and a roof over heads," asked Bill." Well, I can give you a number to some places that will help with bills and food and what evers that you might need." Answered the doctor.

After amitting Bill into the hospital, and got him settled down, Teresa, and the two boys said I good byes and good nights. They left the hospital, and headed home to were Linda and Bill Bill was waiting.

Meanwhile, back at the trailer, Linda and Bill Bill was trying to atural up the living room, and kitchen. As, Teresa and the two boys pulled up the drive way, Linda was in the middle of doing the laundery. When Teresa entered the trailer, she called for Linda and Bill Bill to come into the living room. When they came into the living room, Teresa told them that I father will have to stay for acouple of days, and that she might just need Linda's and Bill Bill's help with James, Bobby, and Joseph. Linda, and Bill Bill said simultaneously," yes ma'am."

For the next few days, Linda and Bill Bill and James did what they could to help around the house. Then one evening the phone rang, Teresa came running to the phone. When she picked up the phone, she asks," hello?" The person on the other end answers," This is the doctor at the Fort Myers emergency hospital. Iam calling you to inform you that you may pick up Bill tomarrow morning." As Teresa and the kids came to the hospital, Linda felt a little qizzy to her tummy. As if she knew that they won't be getting any good news.

When they entered Bill's room, the doctor was all ready there. The doctor trun to Teresa and said," you must be Teresa." Teresa replied," yes sir I am. So whats the atural?" The doctor answers," Well as you all ready know your husband isn't getting better. So, I gave him some pills togive him some confort. Now like I told him, and Iam going to tell you. Make sure he takes these as they are aturalg ok." Teresa replies," yes sir I'll do every thing I can." With that, the doctor handed the checkout papers to Teresa. As doing so Bill started to get out of the wheel chair, then the doctor said," no sir, you get back in the chair. You will have to be pushed out or you can push your self out. Ethir way you will have to stay in that chair till you leave the building." With a smile Bill said," ok doc. What ever you say. When Bill started to roll out of the room, some of the nurses saw him coming and truned I backs to the wall.

As the family was coming to the exit. Bill saw a nurse that didn't see him coming. He first truned to Bill Bill and said," watch this.' Bill started to pick up speed in his wheel chair and lightly let the tire pick up static electric throught his socks. As he came close enough to the nurse,he stuck out his finger and atural the nurse on her behind. The nruse jumped a little with the look of surprise on her face. Every one laughfed, except for Teresa. She told the nurse how sorry she was for his atural, and how he's leaving today. The atur just smiled as she started to relaxs, and said I ok and went on to her dutys. As the hole family retruned home, they all at pizza and watched a movie and settled down for the night.

A couple of weeks to a month later, Linda and Barbra Adams got into a fight that was stupid and fewtile. A few words were exchanged. After being atural by Barbra's choice of words, Linda told Bill Bill to go get I father. By the time Bill Bill made it in side, Linda all ready had Barbra in a choke hold. In that instant Barbra has biten down on Linda's side. As Linda squeezed Barbra's neck, Barbra was biting harder on Linda's side. By that time Bill came rushing out with nothing on but his bathroom atur rapped around his waist. Bill order them both to let go. Then they did as they were told. Bill asked," what the hell is going on here?" As Linda tried to explain her self, Barbra decided to through some more sllers. Bill told Linda to go into the house to change from her church dress to some street clothes. Linda did as she was told. When Linda went into the bathroom to change her clothes, she noticed the bite marks on her side, and knows that Barbra has gotten more of her blood in her system. While wiping the blood off, Linda thought how it was a big mistake it was in I Barbra her blood sister. After the Linda changed her clothes, Linda went back out side. When Linda saw her dad, He had all ready removed Barbra's little sister from her arms. Bill then Looked at Linda and told her to finish what she had finished. By the time Linda went towards Barbra, Barbra grabed her little sister back and started to run home.

After that day Linda never seen or heard from Barbra again. Untill that that night, when there was a knock on the door. Linda and Bill Bill ran to the window to see who it was. As Bill open the door, Linda and Bill Bill was aturalg to each other," it's Barbra's dad and his friends." When Bill saw who it was and why they were there, her truned to Teresa to go get back up I may need it. When Bill took a step out side and shuts the door, Teresa quickly and atural went out the back door. She went couple trailers down to were Jesse, and Boe lived.

Meanwhile, Bill was trying to talk to these atura. When one of them took a swing at him. Bill saw him coming at the corner of his eyes. When he saw the swing, Bill quickly moved back which in trun, causeing him to hit one of his friend. The man replied," *hey you mother fucker you hit me!"* Then Bill replied," *I didn't hit you. If I would've hit you, you'll be on the ground mother fucker. For your information, your dum fuck friend over here hit you!"* As soon as one of them guy started up the porch, Boe came up the walk way saying, "*what the fuck is going on here?"* Some one in the crowd said," *fuck off man this dosen't concern you skinny.""yes the fuck it dose, I my brother in law your fucking with,"* atural Boe. Within that instant Jesse came around the other corner and said," *hay you get your ass off that step before I knock you off!"* When Barbra's father and his friends saw Jesse comeing, they took off. After the intruders left in a hurry, Bill, Jesse, and Boe went in side and started about what happen.

Bill told the other two," I know why they left. They left because, they know I hit like a hammer." Boe replied, "Naw, Bill they ran because, they saw my two guns coming around the corner." Bill and Jesse laughfed at the idea of what Boe had said." Jesse spoked up and said Man you can't scare a cat on Halloween. I'll tell you why they ran. They ran because, they saw my good lookin six pack with hugh guns." Bill and Boe cracked up and they both said," what six pack you only have two and they bounce like boobs, on a Saturday night." After all the jokes were as side and thing begun to calmed down, Jesse, and Boe went home.

Two days latter Linda made a new best friend, and her name was Penny Candy Parr. Linda thought a lot of Penny. To Linda, Penny was older and cool, best of all some one that new how to have fun. Penny had a younger brother named Gersiom Parr. Linda thought this was great, at least some one for Bill Bill to play with, Besides driving Linda crazy. Penny and Linda had sleepovers and atural parties, wich was fun to do. Penny in some way, made Linda forget her problems. They shared every thing together. The fun part of I friend ship, is that they discovered that I intals spelled out PCP, and LSD.

After a month of friendship Penny asked Linda if she could date Bill Bill in secret. Frist Linda said," eeewww gross, I you not me." As she laughed. Then Linda thought how funny it was for a 6th grader to be dateing a 3rd grader, but didn't put to much thought into it.

Then all the sudden, with no warning Linda could hear her dad walking vigrulessly up and down the hall way.

Linda sat up in bed trying to understand what was going on. Linda I to bring her self to her door way, so she could peek out the door. Before she could reach the door way, her father started to scream," *get the fuck out of my house, and away from my daughter! You son of bitch did you hear me! I said get the fuck away from my daughter, and get the fuck away from my house!!*" When Linda heared this, she slamed herself down on her mat and throw her blanket up over head.

The next morning, Linda brought her self into asking her mother what happened last night. Teresa replied," your father was sleep walking, and all I could do is wait till his emoitoins passed before I could guide him back to bed." Linda asked," why didn't you just wake him up?" Teresa responded," because, you can't just wake up a sleep walker, that would kill them." After everyone was atural that every thing was ok,Linda and her brothers pretty much spend most of I time with I friends.

The year was begging to come to an end. The air of the night sky was becoming warm and crisp. Which was unusal for the season at hand. This night ofcourse was silence, not a sound any were. Until Linda was wakened by the red, white, and blue lights. Linda got up, out of bed and opened her door to the hallway. As she walked throught the hall way to the kitchen, she saw her father being rolled out of the trailer on a streacher, and into an ambalunce. Linda fell over onto the floor into tears crying. Linda sarted to scream, "*DADDY, DADDY, DADDY!!!*" Her mother saw Linda crying, and came running to her. She held Linda tight into her arms and I to calm her down. "Linda, please calm down every thing is gonna be alright I promise. But, you got to clam down befor you wake your brothers," begged Teresa. Wipeing the tears from her face Linda replied," yes mam." With that Teresa truned Linda around and leaded her back to bed. As Teresa tucked Linda back to bed, Teresa told Linda," when you wake up in the morning, make sure your brothers got to school and you stay home to watch Bobby, and Joseph ok." Linda slowly nodded her head yes as she drifted off to sleep.

As the new day came, Linda did as her asked. When ever Linda has finished making pancakes, she went to the boy's room and woke them up. As the two got up to take a bath, the other two ate breakfast. After Bill Bill, and James left for school,

Linda asked Bill Bil to tell her the teacher what had happened. Bill Bill replied," sure after all we do go to the same school."

All that day Linda did all the house chores. Linda did the dishes, vacume the floor, and made all the beds in each room. After that, Linda decieded to try to do the clothes. When Linda got all the colors in the washing machine, and going, the phone rung. Linda ran back in the trailer from the back porch, to answer the phone. On the other end of the phone was here father. In atural Linda asked," how are you daddy?" Bill replied in a slow atural voice," I am fine. How are you Linda?" Linda answers in a calmer voice," I am ok daddy." Her father then continued," Linda I want you to do me a favor scences I won't be home for awhile."" Sure dad I will, what is it?", asked Linda. "I want you to take care of your mother and your brothers. Can you do that for me?" asked Bill. "Yes sir, you know I would any day." Replied Linda. After Linda and her father said I good byes, Linda hung up the phone, and finished what she was doing.

After a couple hours later Linda's mother entered the door. Teresa asked," what have you been doing?" Linda replied," I did the house chores for you mom." Teresa also asked," did any one call as I was out." Before Linda could answer the phone rung once again. Teresa went to answer the phone. The phone call was very brief. Teresa grabed the keys, and headed out the door. Before Linda could get a but in or other wize. Teresa truned to Linda as she got in the car and said," as soon as I find out any thing I'll let you know ok." All Linda could do was at her head and gave as slight smile to her mother.

An hour has gone by and Bill Bill, and James came home. When the two boys came in the door, they saw that I mother and father wasn't there. Bill Bill asked," Linda did mom come home yet?" Linda replied," no bub she's not here. She was here, but she left after five minutes later." Bobby asked as he came running out of the bed room," what are we I for supper?" Linda looked at Bobby in the eyes and said," I don't know bubba, but I'll find something ok. Bobby just smiled and said," ok."

When Linda put some hotdogs in a pot with water, her mother walked in the trailer. Linda stared at her mother for a few moments. Teresa looked up at Linda from the couch. When Linda saw the look on Teresa's face, Linda gave a hair crulling scream, and ran to her room. Which caused the boys to come running into the living room. When they saw I mother crying they asked," whats the matter mom?" Teresa replied in sobs," your father is dead." Joseph asked while crying," how did that happened?" Teresa commented still in tears," he did with liquid in his lungs. They couldn't get it all out." Bobby asked," how did that happened? Did he drowned in a tub of water, or sumthin?" "No, nothing like that son," responded Teresa. As she continued," Look a atural body is only made up with so much water and when that has no were to go. It has to go some where, and when it whent there. They couldn't get it out fast enough ok." Bill Bill asked," what aminute I thought the cancer was killing him." Teresa told Bill Bill," son what do you think what was bloking the atural flow of the water in his body?" Bill Bill hung his head low as his brothers were crying and sobbing all over the trailer. When Bill Bill walked passed Linda's bed room, he noticed that she wasn't crying any more. Infact he cault her more like eves dropping on I conversation. Bill Bill asked Linda if she is ok. Linda replied, "yea bub I am ok." Bill Bill continued to his room.

Chapter 7
THE BIG MOVE

It's time for the funeral, and Linda was lagging behind every one. Slowly walking up the stairs to the parlor. Linda saw so many people that she didn't even know, and a few that she did. When Linda entered the parlor she heared her mother crying while holding her baby brother. Bill Bill and James were in the front left role, poking fun at people as they walked by. Linda pointed at them, as, to say stop that you two. Finally Linda made her way to the casket not realizing it. When see looked down at the face that seemed to be only as sleep. Linda tryied to tell her self that this was only a bad joke. That he is going to jump up, and say," GOTCHA ! "But alas,he didn't. When Linda noticed his visable ntilr. Linda knew that it is real, and that he is really is her father in the casket. Linda begun to cry, but then she stoped her self. Only letting a single tear fall, Linda promised not to cry. She knew she couldn't just cry. Linda had to be brave, and strong for her family. Linda just couldn't break down for anything. Linda notce a hair out of place on her fathers head. She ntilr to put a little spit on her finger, and run it down. When Linda went for another round, she went all the way back. To Linda's ntilre, she felt some thing in the back of his head. It felt like ntilre. Before Linda could stop her self another tear fell. Linda said," no more tears, "to her self in a whisper. Linda didn't want to cry any more, unless there were no way out of it. Linda wanted to ask why were there ntilre in back of her fathers head, but then she thought no one would belive her that they were there.

After the third day, the family whent to the grave sight, and put Bill Willaim Malphrus to rest. They put him in between Billy Joe Malphrus, his son, and Elizabeth Metts, his grandmother. Down from them was a horse shoe drive. With a small maintance building in the middle of the grave yard. Before Bill died he had bought a double harted head stone. But, all the family could do and ntil was a plack for him, which was at least decsent.

School has restarted, and winter break has ended. Linda has to finish the fith grade at Sun Coast Elementary. The friends that she thought was friends, weren't. Eventhough every thing seemed straight, wasn't. Linda was beginning to feel betrade by her family, and friends. Linda's ntil was beginning to over welm her, and was feeling angery with every one that crossed her path. Exspeacailly with the voice in her head I constandly nagging at her. All it could say is "it's your fault that every thing is wrong," then laughf about it. Eventhough, Linda knew that it wasn't. Linda was so ntilred that she begun to talk incorherntly. Linda thought she was going crazy.

There she was, kneeling down face frist. Begging it to stop. Linda remembered what a preacher said. The preacher told his congregation," if you feel trapped and you think there is no way out,... call on the Lord. Scream, Jesus please help me. Give me the strength to send this Devil away from me. Then the Lord will give you that strength." This is just what Linda did. When she did she found peace.

Eventhough, Linda was at peace with her self, she knew that the war was far from over. Infact, the fight for her soul and her humanity is far from over. At least for now, Linda could go on with her life. As normally as she can, till she can figure out what is wrong with her, or even why she is the way she is. Some times Linda would just wounder why she is so I from every one els.

Today is a new day and Teresa started to realized that her bills were pilling up on her. Teresa asked all the kids around the table. When all the kids got seated around the table, they all noticed how fidgeity she was. Bill Bill asked," mom whats wrong." Teresa replied," I'm trying to tell you son, that I um. I am going to take a job, and I am going to need y'alls help around here. I don't want any argueing and fighting. We need to help each other till at least we can get these bills caught up. So im taking a job at Mc. Donalds."

While Teresa worked on the weekends, Linda would take care of her brothers, with the help of her best friend Penny of course. When ever Teresa wasn't working, Linda could go on sleep overs at Penny's house having fun all night like 12 year olds should. Then at times Linda would be able to walk to the bus stop with penny from each other's house.

One day Linda thought it would be funny to put lizards on her earlobes and wear them as earrings to the bus stop, so she did. When she got to the bus stop, she asked the "preppy brats" if they liked her earrings. By that time one of the lizards jumped on one of the girl's face, when she screamed and waved her arms all around the lizard went in the girl's mouth. At that time the bus was coming around the corner so Linda pulled the lizard off of her earlobe and put it on a bush ant told it to be good, while Bill Bill, Penny's brother and Penny was on their knees laughing.

After school Bill Bill, Grisom, Penny, and Linda decided to walk home from school by cutting through the woods. When going that way they had to jump the school's back gate, every body made it over but, Linda. Linda's pants has gotten stuck a the top of the gate. Bill Bill started back up the gate, while the other two were laughfing at Linda. When, Bill Bill got to the top, he told his sister to stand on her heels. Linda did as she was told. Linda put her hills in the holes of the gate. As she lifted herself up, Bill Bill tried to unraveled Linda's pants. He ntilre just enough to were Lind started to slip. When Linda begun slipping, she heared her pants tear. Then Linda fell strait to the ground. I, made Penny, Gershiom, and Bill Bill rolling over with laughfter.

After the embarrishing fall, Linda told Bill Bill that they were going strait home. They didn't stop at the coverts to swim or, even to wet them selves. When they made their way home, Linda, and Bill Bill saw I mother's car was home. As they went in side, Linda and Bill Bill saw I mother fast asleep on the couch. Quitely Linda and Bill Bill made I way to I seprate rooms. Quikly Linda changed her ripped pants. When Linda came out of her room, she could hear Bill Bill and the other boys playing the ntil. Linda figured, while they are all in there playing ntil. She would take out the trash, which included her ripped pants. That way her mother wouldn't have to.

Later that day, when Teresa woke up from her nap, she called for her kids to come sit around the table. As the kids gathered around the table, Teresa told her kids," I have something to tell you all. Linda, Bill Bill, James, Bobby Ray, and Joseph sat around the table looking at each other as if to say," what now?" Teresa said in a strong voice," by the end of this school year were moving in with your Aunt Debby." Joseph asks, "why mom, what happened?" Teresa replies," because I can't get these bills cault up by my self, and your Aunt Debby needs help too. So, we figured just maybe we can help each other ok." All the kids said at the same time, "yes mam,"

By the end of the year, Linda has graduated to the 6th grade. Linda was very excited about it. On the last day of school, Sun Coast had a small graduation party in the lunch room. Parents are welcomed to join I children, but like always her parents all ways has so kind of ntil for not intending. Atleast this time Linda's father had a very good reason, he's dead. Like ntil her mother just too buzzy to come. Ethier way Linda didn't let it bother her. She still had a great time at the party, all by her self.

After awhile, Linda had to use the rest room. The rest room was located just across the main office, and right down the lunch room. When Linda came out the restroom, she could hear two other kids talking about pictures. When they spotted Linda, they asked Linda to get I pictures for them. Not thinking Linda went to do what the girls asked of her. While Linda was I she thought," well sences I am here, I probably go ahead and get mine too.

After the party, everyone is getting loaded onto busses. While headed home, Linda was amiring her picture. Then Linda heard some one ask," did you get your graduation picture?" Then some one els replies," Naw man, you have to pay for it." When Linda heard this, she hit her self in the side of the head and said," duh." Linda then thought," oh well my mother need a new picture anyway. She deserves it."

By the time Linda got home, Linda gave her mother the picture that she got from school. When Teresa took the picture, She was really happy to have gotten it. Teresa said," thank you very much Linda. I needed this." Linda replies," your welcome mom." With a smile across Linda's face, she went to her room to start putting every thing in there place.

Afew moments later Bill Bill, James, Bobby, and Joseph came in the door drity. Teresa saw how muddy they were, and ordered them to take a bath. After the boy's bath, Teresa told all the kids to start packing I belongings. Linda stuck out her head into the hall way and said," I've all ready started."

The next day, Aunt Debby came over to see if there were anything that she could help with. Teresa repies," yea sis, maybe you could load up some of Bills old stuff for me ok." Debby answers," sure sis, I can do that." While Debby was doing what her big sister asked, Teresa was trying to load up the pictures in the living room, along with the nicknacks that was left on the shelfs. Teresa Called for Linda to see if she was done. Linda answers," yes mam, all my stuff is in the van." Teresa asked," Linda can you help Debby and my self in the kitchen?" Linda replies," yes mam." When Debby went the boy's room, she wanted to see if there were any thing left in I room. Then I way back Teresa asked," were is the floor?" In laughfter, Debby asked," do you mean were is the broom?" Linda told her aunt," the broom is be hind you." Debby resured Teresa, that it was ok, and that every one makes mistakes when they are stressed.

When every thing was loaded up in Debby's truck and Teresa's van, they were ready to go. Linda started to think about Penny. Linda begged her mother if she could go over Penny's house to say good bye. Teresa told Linda," yea you could tell Penny good bye. But, you aint walking over there, we'll drive ok.

After Linda, and her little cousins, Kathy, and Wahneta loaded up in the van, Bill, James, and Bobby loaded in the back of the pick up. While Joseph, and Leo road with Debby in the front of the pick up. As they begun to drive away from Sun Coast, Linda reminded her mother to stop at Penny's house. As they stoped at Penny's house, Teresa told Linda," you only have 15 minutes." As Linda slamed the door, she replies," yes mam."

When Linda walked up to the door, she knooked on the door. Penny's mom, When Linda open the door, Linda asked," may I go see Penny. Linda answers," sure, go right ahead. She's in her bed room." As Linda walked into the house, she took off her shoes. After all it was house rules. Then Linda went into Penny's room. When Penny looked up at Linda, Penny asked," whats wrong Linda?" Linda looked at Penny with tears slowly running down her eyes and said," were moving." Penny in shock of the news and said," what, when?" Linda replies," were moving, right now." Penny got up from her bed with tears running down her face also and said," oh no, man I not right!" Linda answers," I know, right!" Penny asked," well we still be friends?" Linda replied," always, remember, LSD, and PCP, friends forever. Penny said with a ackward smile," I'll remember, friends forever.

A I seconds later Bill Bill came into the room and said," Linda lets go, every one is waiting on you. Then Bill Bill smiled at Penny and said," were's Grisom?" Penny replies," gone with my dad," Bill Bill also asked," ok then, can you tell him good bye for me?" Penny told Bill Bill," yea I'll tell him." Bill Bill ntilr tugged on Linda's shoulder and said," lets go, they'er waiting for us!" Linda replies in ntilredn," I know, I know give me a minute already!" Penny and Linda gave each other I last hugs and good byes befor leaving Penny's room. After Linda, and Bill Bill loaded back up in I places, the family left Sun Coast to live some were new.

As the family moved to Aunt Debby's house, Linda noticed the big back yard. Past the yard was a road. On the other side of the road was a church. "At least I can still go to church," thought Linda.

On the first night in a strange place, it was wet and cool. The rain and lighting was seen through the window. As the lighting strikes, Linda can see the weeping willow blowing in the wind in the distance. Then all the sudden, out of the blue. As the lighting strikes, Linda could see some one, or some thing stareing in at her in the window. Linda didn't dare to look away, or yell for help. Linda didn't know what to do. She was ntil from the site of it. All Linda did was just stared right back at it, till she fell asleep. All Linda could I saying to her self right befor falling asleep was," man this thing is ugly. It looks like something between the living dead and a demon."

The next morning, Linda got up and got dressed. After getting dressed, Linda ran strait out side. As she came around the corner of the house, Linda could hear her brothers moveing around. When Linda went further around the house, she came to her bed room. Linda looked all around the ground for ntilr of foot prints, or just anything to prove that she isn't crazy. After awhile Linda gave up looking, and thought," maybe I just dreamed it."

A week later, Linda's other cousins came over for a vist for a few days. On the first day, all the adults asked all the kids to find a place to take 30 minute to nap. All the kids agreed to the nap, and tried to lie down for awhile. All except for Linda, and Kathy, Aunt Debby's oldest child. Linda, and Kathy was restless. They just couldn't rest. So, they just ntilred back and forth to each other. When Linda tried to wisper a story back to Kathy, they both heared a strange noise. Soon as they heard the noise, they both lied down very quickly, pulling blankets over I head.

When Linda and Kathy layed very stillmon the bed, asif to pretending to be asleep. Then out of no were Linda got hit hard on her back. At the shock of the hit Linda stayed motionless a few more moments longer. After a few mintues gone by, Linda slowly moved to her side and moved the blanket from her head. Were Linda was lieing down at, she could see her cousin's face. Kathy gave Linda the same look, as if some one struck her in from behind also. As Kathy and Linda slowly looked around the room they came to realized that something wasn't right.

On the second day, every thing was pretty quiet, ntil that night came. All the kids were in one room. The kids decided to tell scary stories. The eldest cousin said," I bet if we stare at the closet door. You can still see an arm reaching out to us, but frist we'll have turn off the lights." Everyone els said," ok." Most of them figured that the one missing cousin was in the closet.

Chapter 9
DENILE

So, everyone stared at the door. Then suddenly, very slowly the closet door came open. Then you could barely see a hand coming out of the door. At first, it was the fingers wrapped around the edge of the door. Then, the hand feeling it's way around the door. Next was the arm came out from behind the door. Then, it started to reach out to the kids sitting on the top bunk of the bunk bed. Right before any one could see the shoulders, the lights came on. To I ssigned, the one missing cousin came I door. The younger cousins screamed, and when the adults came rushin they asked," whats the hell going on." When Leo, and Whaneta blurted out a gost in the closet. Unlce Bill flung open the closet door and said," look there is no gost, boogy man, or golblin in the closet, There never was, and never will be. Now cut it out." Then the younger kids begun to cry. Teresa told all the kids," the younger ones can take the adult's bedroom, and the older ones sleep in the living room. While Debby, and I take the kid's bed room, and I'll prove to you that there isn't any gosts.

That very morning, Teresa, and Debby told all the kids to pack up and get ready to move again. Debby moved in with the guy she was dateing, while Teresa moved in with her Aunt Betty. Aunt Betty was recently dateing a man named Roy, which she had a date with that night at a local bar. Aunt Betty asked Teresa if she wanted to go along. Teresa replied," not if it means iam gonna be the ssig wheel." Aunt Betty told Teresa," ok. Then how about if I ask Debby, and your mom along. Would you come then?" Teresa replied," sure, then I'll come along."

When the adults decieded to leave, they left Linda in charge of her brothers, and five cousins. While the grown ups were gone. The kids plaied hide and seek in doors. When that got boreing, they all sat around and colored for ssign. After some of the younger cousins fell asleep, the others told gost stories. The kids sat around in a circle and begun to tell tier stories. Bill Bill told stories about robots, while James told stories about gosts, and Anthony talked about killer birds. Linda mainly spoke about vampires. Right before Linda heared the grown ups pulling up the drive way, she told another story about Bloody Mary. As the front door opened up Linda ssigned to the kids," hurry, get in bed we shouldn't been up this late." Anthony ssigne to go to bed. When Aunt Betty saw that Anthony was still up, she was sore with Linda. When Aunt Betty was done scalding Linda, Linda then truned to Anthony and said, It's ok I'll get even with you!" Anthony replied," oh yea, you and what army."

That very night, just to prove a point that Linda can do surtand things that no one els seems to be able to do. She visted Anthony in his dreams. That following morning Linda askd Anthony," sleep well." Anthony just looked at Linda in ssigned. After awhile Anthony didn't give

Linda any more hard times, and they went to play with the other children.

A week later Aunt Betty got married to Roy at the city park under a cuzzebo with a lake in the distance. Linda thought that it was I. As Linda was looking around, she noticed that her mother, and a couple of her aunts, and one uncle came up missing. After the wedding, Aunt Betty was now Mrs., and Mr. Roy Roberts. As they begun to leave for I hunnymoon, they saw I car all dressed up with JUST MARRIED acrossed the back window. Aunt Betty found her underware tied to the antanna of the car, and said," ha ha very funny. As she started to untie it, Roy laughfed and said," no leave it, it's funny." Then they got in the car and drove away with cans tied to the bumper.

As Linda wached them drive away, Linda had a cold chill run down her spine. Then when she thought about her mother, another cold chill ran down her spine followed by a vision of red shoes. Afterwards, Linda heared laughfter in the slite breeze of the wind. Linda looked around and it seemed asif no one ssigned it. Linda sighed to her self and said in a wisper," oh boy not again."

One night after the hunny moon of Roy and Betty Roberts, Betty decieded to go out with the girls to a bar. Were Roy would meet Betty so, that way they could role play. Which Betty said to Linda," we will be gone for a while, and that WE WILL be back. So, make sure every one is asleep at I bed times. Linda replied," yes mam."

Linda wathed over her brothers and cousins again. Linda's brothers,and her cousins agreed with Linda, and to just hang out around the house till the grown ups come back. Ofcourse, Linda didn't think that they would be gone this long. Linda thought she might have to fix some kind of snack for them to eat. Linda didn't know what, or, how to fix it. So, she whent to the kitchen to see what she can find. Linda found some hot dogs, and chips. When it was done, Linda told the rest of them what she had. Everyone said," yea, we'll eat that."

As it begun to reach 9:00 pm, Linda told all the kids that it had reached I bed time. All the kids whent to bed, except Anthony. He asked Linda if he could stay up a little longer. Linda replied," sure, you aint but a year yunger than me anyway." Anthony staied up to keep Linda company. But, Anthony couldn't stay up for too long, and then he fell asleep. Linda had to wake him up just to lead him back to his bedroom, to finish going to sleep. Linda then returned to the couch in the living room. After awhile, Linda noticed that it was working on 2:00 am. Linda was I to worry.

Then all the sudden Linda heared a car door slam shut. Linda peered out of the window from that was behind the couch. Linda saw her mother drunk and stumbling everywere saying," I am so hot." Then she takes off her top, as, she jumped into a kiddy pool. Linda just shook her head, as she went to her bed. While Linda was in her bed, as she begun to think about her dad. Linda, remembered the time her family moved into a trailer park, while living in a camper. Then she thought about how her father came home drunker then, a skunk on a ssigned candy. She remembered how her father pulled up at the trailer, and falling out of the truck door The way Bill Bill, James, and

Linda laughfed at him as she stumbles his way into the door way. How her mother tries to help him to bed, and all he wanted to do is tell Teresa how he ran over a stop sign. How he was slurring his words as he talks.

As, Bill Bill on top bunk, looks down at his mother and asks," whats the matter with dad?" Teresa replies," he's drunk." Bobby, Down at Linda's feet, on bottom bunk, looks and lefts his head, and says," is that what a drunk man looks like?" Teresa replies," yes it dose, and if you don't want to look like an idiot, then don't get drunk." Linda rolling over getting Joseph off of her, replies with her other brothers," yes mam." As, Bill begun to puke, Teresa grabed a trash bag. While Teresa was getting a bag for Bill, Linda was able to see her father. Lida saw how red in the face he was, and how his eyes are blood shot." When Bill saw Linda, he said," LLLLinda gggo to ssssleeep ok." Linda replied with s ssig smile," yes sir." Then Linda rolled over toward Joseph, and whent to sleep.

That morning, when Linda, Bill Bill, and James went to the busstop, they saw that the stop sign was really down on the grown. Even though the buss was in sight, The three really didn't say to much to each other but," wow!" After school Teresa sat down all the kids and explained to them," the only reason I father came in drunk last night was because, he was fired from his job, and that he misses Billy Joe very much." The kids looked at each other and said," yes mam."

A couple weeks later, Teresa anoucese that she now has a boy friend, and that he could be the one. Linda and Bill Bill asked I mother at the same time, who is he ? What is his name?" Teresa replies," his name is Junior Green." Bobby asks," what dose he do?" Tersa replies," he picks fruit."

The kids got together to come up with a scime to get rid of this guy too. One day, a man showed up at the front door. When Roy whent to open the door, this guy inrduced himself as Junior Green. Roy opened the door more to let him inside. When Junior entered the house, Roy told every one who he was. As time went by, Junior asked if Teresa was ready for I date. Teresa replies," yea, iam ready. Just let me get my pocket book. After Teresa, and Junior left the house, Roy truned to Betty and said," I think that boy is gay."

Couple days later, Junior started coming over more often. All the kids begin to notice how Junior was walking, talking, and holding his self up. One day Anthony told Junior," man, yor gay." Junior in ssigned answers," what did you say." Anthony said," you heared me. Your gay aren't you." Junior denies that he was gay. Then Anthony started to argue with Junior, while Bill Bill cut in and said "you argue like a girl, so obviously you are gay." Junior then implied," hey, I was rasied by my mother most of my life." Bill Bill asks," didn't you have friends that were boys?" Junior replies as he has become angered," YES I DID!" Anthony then impies with a cricket smile on his face," yea, he sure did, BOY FRIENDS!" All the kids begun to point and laugh at Junior. Junior got really up set and left for awhile.

While Junior was gone, everyone tried to tell Teresa about Junior, but she didn't listen and soon moved in with him when he got the job in Fort Myers. While they were in Fort Myers and school started back, Joseph started kindergarten and went to school with James and Bobby, while Linda and Bill Bill went to school together. Linda was excited to show Bill Bill around middle school.

One day when Bill Bill and Linda came home from school, their mom and Junior was not there so they've decided their mom was working late. Later, when the other kids got home from school, their mom came home with pizza and apologized for being out so late explaining the hours of working in watermelons, so they all said okay.

After 3 months they all moved to South Bend, Indiana; Linda and Bill Bill noticed that Junior was acting very strange(and not the gay way), which meant something was not right with their mom and Junior. Infact, their mother quit buying food for the house causing the kids to go hungry. So Linda asked the boys if they wanted to go to work in people's yard to make food money, and they thought it was a great idea.

The next day after school, Linda, Bill Bill, and James got some black bags, and went to work. They were paid $3.00 an hour. Even though, it only took about 30 minutes to 10 minutes most of the time. This was when Linda really knew what it means to work for what she wanted. Even if it was just for snacks to last during the day.

After awhile, Bill Bill gave up and James made a old woman to be his friend. She had a daughter that would bring him some chicken from where she works. So everyday he would go to the lady's house to get chicken to eat. For the rest of the time in South Bend, Linda would work all by her self. Until one day soon after school was out, two great big men were arguing with Junior(they called him Robert Green). They were saying if he didn't have their money they would kill him; Linda thought to herself 'he borrows money from stupid people, but yet no food in the house what a retarted faggit.'

After the two men left, Junior told Teresa," tell your kids to hurry up and pack up. We got to go now." Teresa did as she was told. Linda ask," why did those men call Junior, Robert?" Teresa replies," because, I his name." Linda thought, 'well then, I what I'll call him too. Besides Robert suites him better."

While, every one got loaded up into the car, and drove away, Linda was able to hear Robert wisper to Teresa," man I close. Iam glad we got away with our skin still attached." Bill Bill asks," were are we going now?" Robert told Bill Bill," were going to West Virgina."

While going through the bottem part of West Virgiana, Linda was looking out of the window. Linda thought, what a beautiful state. It had some hills, but mostly holler down sides of, clifes of ssigned. Linda has never seen such perfectl shaped pine trees. Linda thought they looked like nacked christmass trees.

Finally they all stoped at a ridge, which had a long ssig driveway that leaded to the left. Then whent to the right again. At the end of the drive way was a quint little house. There lived in that house was Robert's uncle, a cousin, and his cousins two sons.

Up the walk way, Linda noticed that the little house looked old and worn down. The yard was dark with the shadows of large trees all around the property. There were hardly any flowers, just lots of weeds. As Linda walkd into the house, she saw how trashed the house really was. There were clothes and trash every were. Dishes packed with food, and some with magits on sink counters. Empty pizza boxes on the floor and tables. Linda thought, how disgusting. I can't belive that were gonna live like slobs.

After kicking things around in Linda's ssigned room, Teresa came into the room. Teresa asked," Lindawill you help me to clean up the kitchen so we could start super?" Linda replied," yes mam." Two hours of cleaning the kitchen, they finally had it fit to cook food in. After super was done Teresa, and Linda tackled the living room and bathroom. When the cleaning was done Linda was worn out, she didn't even feel like cleaning her bed. Linda just nocked every thing onto the floor and fell asleep on a nacked bed.

That morning Linda got up tp shower, and get ready for the bed. As linda came into the living room Teresa told all the kids to get ready to be signed up for school again. On the way to the schools, Linda begun to notice the ride was dragging along. Finally they came to the high school, and Teresa signed up Linda first. When they was finished with Linda, they started on Bill Bill. Right when the school got half way through with Bill Bill, they realized that he needs to be in the elementary. This news sadden Linda. She was looking forward to having Bill Bill in the same school again. This year Joseph gets to start kindergarding.

Chapter 11
DRUNKIN CUPID

After signing up for school, Linda found out she would have to ride two buses to and from school. When school did start, Linda noticed couples walking around holding hands, and giving google eyes again. Linda tried to not notice how I she was. When she did, Linda thought to her self, no one isn't ever gonna notice me, or care for me at all. All Linda knew was, it only seems that the only time any one took notice, is when they think they could get some thing from her,or just think she's easy. Which wasn't right at all. Linda just orrifi to be a loner.

Every time Linda finally gets home it's all ready so late it's dark out side. By the time Linda finishing doing her chores, it was time to eat and take a bath. Then be ready for bed for the night. When this hole season got going rel good, Linda begun to feel orr and unhappy again. There was orrifieds falling over Linda. Then one day out of aggravation, Linda snapped at Robert, and begun to curse him. Robert begun to yell back at Linda, while Teresa hide in the kitchen. For curseing Robert, Linda had to be punished, and for that the concenquin was for Linda to miss school. Linda told Robert," you are so stupid. I have heared any body to be grounded from school." Robert told," Linda tomarrow instead of going to school, your going to work with your mother and my self." Linda looked at Robert with orrifi in her eyes.

The next day when Linda got up, she got her brothers up for school like she all ways did. Then she would get her self dressed. After Linda got dressed, she tried to sneak off to school. As Linda tried to open the front door Teresa asked," Linda are you about ready for work?" Linda replies," for you maybe, for him no!" "For me, Linda so I don't have to hear the bitchin," begged Teresa. "Ok then, I will for you mom," answers Linda. Linda whent ahead to the car to work in the apples.

As Robert, Teresa, and Linda drove out to the apple I, Linda once again notice how beautiful the country side was. With the fog hanging around the tops of the orrified. Linda loved the crisp air, and the freshness of the scent too. Linda also loved how shadey every thing was. The sun didn't bother her so much.

When they reached the apple I, Robert gave Linda a sack to ground hog the apples from the bottom of the tree. Linda whent to the nearest apple tree, and started to slam the apples in her sack. When Teresa heared the way Linda was picking the apples, she told Linda not to be picking the apples like that. When Linda asked," why not, all he's goona do is throw the bags in the trunk and leave'em be till next time." Teresa replies," no he won't ether, because he'll check'em and if they are nasty he'll bitch at me and then we'll have to clean them up." "Ok mom, I'll pick them a little softer then." Answers Linda as she rolls her eyes.

As the day ended, Robert, Teresa, and Linda loaded up to go back to the house. Like always Linda notice how every thing looks I at dusk. As Robert took the sharp truns aroud the cliffs, Linda would grip the sides of her seat and door panel. Some times Linda would even orrif her teeth in fear off going over the side.

When Robert, Teresa, and Linda finally made it back to the house, Linda would briskly walk to her room and shut the door, After shutting the door, Linda locked it, as she crashed on her bed in relief. Moments later Teresa was nocking at the door. When Linda got up to let her mother in, Linda could hear Robert running his mouth. After Teresa gained enternce, she told Linda, Robert wants me to yell at you, for yelling at him, and cursing him the way you did." Nothing new mother, you will always do what that dope head fagot say's, so go ahead yell at me. But I am gonna say this, if he wants me to curse him, then I will. I'll curse him with the most hurifcate pain and orrified manageable. Then he'll orrifi how lonely he really is." Teresa just looked at Linda in orrifie. She didn't know what to say. As,Linda continued," I am so tired of him. Even when some one tries to tell you some thing, and it seems that all your in love with is Robert. Exspecially, when one of your kids try to tell you the truth about that dope head brain dead. Teresa felt bad about the hole thing I been going on. Teresa hung her head low as she lifted her self up off Linda's bed, and left the room.

Couple months went by, the apple season was over. Robert told the family," well, it's time to go back to florida." In a strage way, Linda hated the idea of leaveing West Virgina. Linda just loved how beautiful this state is. As all ways, Linda and Teresa packed up the vehicle to get ready to go back to Florida.

After getting back to Wahneta, Florida, Robert dragged every one to his friend's house. While there, Robert was talking to a man named Richard. When junior was done talking, he came back to Teresa and said," we can stay here till the watermelons start real good." Teresa replies," ok." While unloading the car. Linda, and Bill Bill ask," where in the world are we going to sleep?" Teresa replies," the boys are going to sleep in the living room. Sheila is sleeping in Richard's room. Robert, and I am gonna sleep in Sheila's room, and you are sleeping under the kitchen table." Bill Bill replies," oh", Linda rolls her eyes as she walks away.

A few hours later, Teresa told Linda," why woun't you go out side and get some air." Linda replies," cause, it's to hot out side." Teresa said," it ain't gonna kill ya to go out side, and explore." Linda thought about it for a few minutes and then asks," can Bill Bill, James, and Bobby come with me?" Teresa replies," I kinda the point, now ain't it." As Linda went out the door, she called Bill Bill, James, and Bobby to see if they wanted to go walking. Naturally they said yes. Then Joseph wanted to go to, Linda didn't want to worry with Joseph, with him being so young yet. Linda decided to give the ask mom and slip away rutine.

As Bill Bill, Linda, James and Bobby walked down the road, they noticed a little block church. Linda thougt to her self, well at least I know were I am gonna be on Sunday morning, and nights, not forgetting Wensday nights. When they came to the end of the road, Linda asks," were to next guys." James suggested," lets go to the right."

While they were walking down Rifle Range, Bill Bill noticed a pool hall. All the boys looked at Linda as if to be asking permission to go in side. Linda just sighed and said," lets go in side." When they whent in side they noticed the video games and pinball machines. There was even fresh food, and a few pool tables. Bill Bill, and James asked Linda if she had any money on her. Linda said," yea I do, at least some any way. Why?" Linda pulled out some money from her pockets to count. Bill Bill replies," to play some games." Linda gave her brother a couple of dollars to get change with. Linda sat at the table while watching her brothers play games. Which was something they didn't get to do for a long time.

After awhile, Linda notice how late it was beginning to be. Linda told her brothers that it was time to go back to the hell hole. Bobby laughfed at what Linda had told them. He thought it was funny that his sister said hell hole. After retruning back to the house, Linda saw how Joseph was out side all by his self. When Linda called out for Joseph, he came running to his sister. Linda asked Joseph," how long have you been out side all by your self?" as Joseph looked to the ground, he said," ever scents you left me here." Linda was getting up set. Then she asks Joesph," did you at least tell mom that I left you behind?" Joseph answers," yea, but she act as if she didn't care." Linda then asked," did you have some thing to eat at least?" Joseph then replies," no, not a thing." When Linda was in the middle of asking Joseph another question, Bobby kept tugging at Linda's sleeve. When Linda ask Bobby," what is it?" Bobby pointed at the car port and said," look sis." Linda looked towards the car port, and saw lots of I people in and out of the house. Linda started to have her imagenation at work. Linda couldn't say any thing because she wasn't sure to whats going on.

Later that night, things seems to be quiet down. After supper, Linda told Joseph that for now he could start going every were they went, At least I will now were all my brothers are and if they are ok, thought Linda. That night after every one went to bed, thing begun to get noisey again. Linda couldn't get any sleep. Linda kept hearing a baby cry, and people yelling at each other. This kept on for weeks. After awhile Linda started to put the puzzle together. Linda finally orrifi what was going on.

The next day Linda told her mother that she was going to go for a walk, and she's going to take her brothers with her. When the boys heared what Linda said, they all gathered at the door. One by one the boys went out the door, with Joseph in the rear. When they all made it to the end of the drive way, Linda took Joseph by the hand, so that way he can't get hurt, and proceed to the pool hall.

While at the pool hall, Linda gave Joseph some loose change that she had in her pocket. With a big smile Joseph took the change and whent to the first video game he saw. As Joseph was playing games, Linda and the other boys, sat at a table to talk about whats been going on. First Linda talked about how she thinks that I mother is hooked on drugs, and how that just be the reason that there isn't any food in the house. The boys agreed that it may be the reason for a lot of things. Then Bill Bill talked about how he thinks that Richard may be as gay as Robert. Bobby ask," why do you think that bub?" Bill Bill replies," because, he knew I wasn't as sleep, and he just sat there smileing at me, while he's was jacking off." Bobby started to point and laughf at Bill Bill. James told Bobby," don't do that Bill Bill gonna kick your butt Bobby." Bobby did as james said with a half grin on his face.

After the meeting, Linda called Joseph so they could go home for the day. Three days later, Linda came home from school to see her mom crying. Linda ask," whats the matter mom?" Teresa replies," Junior is in jail and on top of that iam pregnate." With sarcasm, Linda said in a wisper," yea right *his* baby, and on top of that, I bet he went for drugs." Teresa ask," what did you say?" Linda said," what did he go to jail for mom, drugs?" Teresa replies,' funny, but no, he went to jail for not checking with his proll officer." Linda replies," oh." By that time the boys came in from school. When Bill Bill saw how up set his mother looked, Bill Bill ask," whats wrong now?" Linda filled Bill Bill in and told him to explain it to the rest of I brothers. While Bill Bill went to talk to James, Bobby, and Joseph, Linda went to get more information from her mother. Linda ask," what are you gonna do now, mom?" Teresa told Linda," I would have to stay here till the third of the month. Then I'll just see if I could move in with my mother."

That following month, Teresa moved in with her mother on the poor side of LaBelle. Just in time for summer school to end, and regular school to start. Linda thought to her self, well at least this school has a juke box in the lunch room. When Linda was in the lunch room, she would walk up to the stage were the juke box is and slip a quarter in the slot. Linda would then press B12, which was her favoret song. As Linda got half way through lunch, Linda started to notice people holding hands, and saying mushy stuff to each other. Linda got sick to her stomake, and decide to go to the trash area to dump out her tray. As she slide the tray on top of the other trays, Linda notice two other cartons of chocolate milk. While standing there, Linda gone ahead and opened them up and drunk them down within minutes. After throughing away the cartons, Linda went out side to wait for the bell to ring.

While out side, Linda decided to lay back under an old oak tree. With her cap pulled over her eyes, and her boots orrifi over a big root. Linda was confortable, orri this girl came up to Linda, and told her that her friend liked her. Linda pulled her cap up to see who was talking to her. Before Linda could say what, the gir apolized for the mix up. With a funny look on Linda's face, she said that it was alright, and resumed the restful state she once was in.

As the first bell rung, Linda got up from her confrot zone to go stand in line for the next class. While waiting, a boy came to her to as if she wanted to fight, thinking that Linda was a boy. When Linda truned around, he two apolized, and walked away. This was I to make Linda mad. But she then calmed her self, by saying to her self," at least you don't have to worry about any body giving you those stupid google eyes.

After six months of quiet, and feeling safe, Teresa got all the kids orrifie. Teresa told the kids," we're moving back to Wahneta." Linda, and Bill Bill looked at each other and said," what, why?" Teresa reminded them," well, you know I am pregnant and we're married." At the same time Bill Bill and James said," *MARRIED, eeww gross*!" While Linda just looked at her mother with disgust. Linda ask," why in the world would you want to?" Teresa said," I've told you already Linda." Then Linda said," but mom we can help you with the baby, you don't need him." Teresa said scornly," Linda I told you already and I final. Idon't want hear any more about it."

A few days later, Teresa moved back in with Junior. Mean while on the way there Linda, and James orrified to Bill Bill," *ha ha, you better watch out for Richard.*" Then Linda and James started to ask I mother, "are we moving back with Richard?" Teresa told her kids," no, we're moving in Junior's house on 11th street east." Bill Bill asked in curiosty," if junior had his own house, then why did we move in with Richard, at that one time?" Teresa replies, because he had some one living in it, I why." In surprise Linda, and Bill Bill said," oh, ok."

After getting to Wahneta, and got unpacked in a two bed room, and one bath house, Teresa wanted Linda, and the boys to go out side to get some air. After some time Teresa, stepped out side to call the kids in to eat. After eating, and the kitchen was cleaned up, Teresa told her kids to be ready in the morning to be signed up for school. Linda and her brothers did as they were told. They gathered every thing they needed for the next day.

That morning Linda got up early. She got her self showered, and dressed for school. When she got done with her self, she got started on her brothers. Making sure each one was dressed and ready to go to shool. All Linda had to do with Bill Bill, was to makes sure he was dressed decently.

The first school we came to was an elementary, which were Joseph, Bobby, James, and Bill Bill going to. After signing them up, they all whent to the next school in Winter Haven. As they came to the school, it read Denison Middle school. When they entered the school house, Linda noticed the stairs. After the sign up, and getting her schedule, Linda noticed, that she'll be going up and the stairs. As she walked back by the stairs on the way out, Linda wiped her forehead and thought, well at least I'll have plenty of excerzie going up and down all day.

One day after school, Linda came home to find her mother just finishing supper. An hour or two later, Linda's brother were all up set for being hungery. Linda asked her mother if ti was all right for the boys to go ahead and eat. Tereas replies," no, we got to wait for Junior to come in first." Linda went back out side and told her brothers what was said. Joseph moaned, "but were hungery now!" Linda told her brothers," go play ball for awhile, maybe you won't think about it to much."

As the boys went to do what there big sister asked, Robert came in the drive way. As he got out of the car and headed into the door, Linda knew something wasn't right. Linda followed him into the door of the house. As soon as Robert saw Teresa, he begun to make crazy demands. Linda, thought this would be the best time to get some food while the I is good. While Robert and Teresa begun to argue, Linda quickly got a plate and started to pile on the food. When Linda got as much food as she could she snuck the plate out the door without any one noticing.

Afew moments later after Linda hide her plate in an opening in some bricks. Robert came busting out the door hollering how that food wasn't fit for a dog. As Robert dumped out the food to the dog, the boys were screaming at him. When Robert blurted out," I don't have to listen to this crap," and got into his car, and drove away, Linda saw how up set her brothers were. After I mother went in side, Linda orrified for her brother to come to her. When they did, Linda pulled out the plate of food, and told her brothers to start orrif, before Robert gets back. The boys each dove into the plate grabbing what ever they could eat, and shovling it into I mouths as quickly as they could without choking.

Twenty minutes later, Robert came back to the house carring food from a fast food joint. As Robert sat on the couch, he opened up the back and begun to eat. When Teresa asked him for some of the food, Robert grinned and said," this food is for me only you want food go fight the dog." This begun to anger Linda whe she heard him say this to her mother. Linda tried to fight back the feeling of hatered for him. Linda didn't want the voices to come back. The voices are aggervating enough as it were, thought Linda.

A few weeks later, after the oranges was over, Robert moved the family to Immocale, into a trailer, and once again, Linda and her brothers had to resign up for school. In the morning, everything always seems a blurr to Linda. As always, Linda wakes up, takes a shower, fix breakfast for her brothers, and get ready for school. By this time Linda would have to walk a mile to school and home again with Bill Bill at her side.

One day, without thinking, after school, Linda just walked straight home. About thirty minutes later, Bill Bill came in all up set. At the table Bill Bill picked up a tweentyfive percent silver butcher knife, and strated to wave it around. As he came closer to Linda, Bill Bill orrifie," *why didn't you wait for me?*" Linda said," I forgot, I didn't think that you were there. Bill Bill asked as he begun to franicly wave the butcher knife," *when you saw I wasn't there. Why didn't you come back for me?*" When Linda tried to explain, Bill Bill came rushing at Linda. Linda tried to make a dash for the front door. As she flung the door open, Bill Bill came down with the butcher knife. When Linda ran out the door a trickle of blood followed behind her.

A few moments later, the door slamed behind her. When Linda cautionly walked back to the door, she heard the door double locked. As Linda searched for where the blood was coming from, she told her brother how sorry she was for not waiting on him. Through the door Bill Bill replied," yea right, what ever." Then Linda found were the blood was coming from. As Linda tried to bound the wound, Linda told Bill Bill," really I was coming back for you. It's just I was waiting on Bobby and Joseph. I didn't know aczackly when they be home." Bill Bill thought about what Linda said, and unlocked one of the locks, and said, next time wait for me next to the office. Is that a deal for you?" Linda replied," yea, now let me in Bobby and Joseph is coming and I don't want them to see the gash in the back of my arm." In curiousity Bill Bill quickly open the door to see if he really did get his sister. As Bill Bill open the door he asked," sis did I really get you?" When Linda rushed into the front door and orrifie to the bath room she said," yea you did bub."

As Linda ran to the bathroom slamming the door behind her, she quickly trun on the lights, and stood in front of the mirror. While holding the back of her arm closed, Linda was tring to pull off her shirt to take a better look. While staring into the mirror, Linda saw her wound slowly heal it self. When it got down to a slite cut, Linda wrapped a orri around her self, to get a new shirt to put on. After that day, Linda and Bill Bill learnd to respect each other, to help each other when in need. A few weeks later Bill Bill and James found the same understanding.

A month gone by, and Linda was a little behind on house work. She tried everything to catch up, but couldn't. At last it has gotten late, and Robert came in grumpy. As orrif looked around the house, he wiped his two fingers on everything. Then Robert trun to Linda and said," you didn't do a dam thing in this house did you." Linda just swallowed the commets down. Trying to egnore what was being said. Then Robert noticed the kitchen floor wasn't swiped or moped. Walking through the kitchen, Robert shakeing his head, while Linda just following behind him. As Robert poped his head into the door way of the bathroom, he started to complain about the clothes wasn't washed or hung to dry. Linda was getting orrified with Robert, she wanted to tell him how bad she felt. Linda also knew he wouldn't care. After Robert found fault with all the other rooms, he dcieded to check Linda's room.

When Robert got in the room, he started to complain about the bed not being made. Then Robert went to the dresser, and started pulling Linda's clothes out. While Robert pulling Linda's clothes out of the dresser, he begun to yell at her for not folding her clothes, and orrifi them in the dresser. Right when Robert was telling Linda how he was going to throw out her clothes out into the yard, Linda yanked her clothes back from Robert and told him," *don't you think one freakin minute your gonna throw my clothes out the door, like you did my mother's cookin. I ain't my mother your talkin to you dope headed fagot. I swear I'll tell everyone I know what's going on around here if you even think about throwing MY CLOTHES! You might through my mothers cookin out I door but you ain't gonna through my clothes out the door!*"

That night lieing in bed, Linda could hear mumbleing in her mother's room. Linda couldn't quite hear what was said, expecially when she is trying to hear over the voices in her head. Linda thought, what ever it is they are talking about, it ain't good. Linda tried all night long to ignore the voices that was tauting her earilier that day.

After the orrifieds was over, Robert took the family back to Wahneta. Linda once again was inrolled into Denison Middle school, but this time for some reason they sent Bill Bill back to the elementary again. Linda thought, he is just ain't gonna catch a break. Now Bill Bill, James, Bobby, and Joseph are in the same school. After a week back at Wahneta, Robert and Teresa got into a fight. As Linda came walking up to the drive way, her mother was walking out of the drive way crying. Linda started to trun around and follow her mother and ask," what happen, why are you crying?" Teresa said in tears," he hit me!" Linda wasn't really shocked, but she was mad. Linda then noticed that Bobby and Joseph wasn't with them. Linda truned around to Roberts house to recive Bobby, and Joseph.

When she met them at the door steps, Linda looked at Robert with the evil eyes, and said," are you two coming or what?" The two boys just looked at Linda with confusement on I faces. Then Linda said," let me put it this way. Are more scared of me or him? If it's me, then come on now." Before Linda could finish her I, the two boys ran to me I mother. Before Linda could leave also, for some odd reason Linda took another step closer to Robert and said something in a language that no one new. Then Linda was able to walk away from Robert. As Linda was catching up with her mother, Linda was trying to figure what in the world she just said, and were did it came from, while the same time the voices in her head was laughing.

By the time Linda cault up with her mother, Teresa was in the middle of a phone call. The person on the other in was telling her mother to go back and try to make things right. When Teresa agreed with this notion, Linda was orrified. After Teresa hung up the pay phone at Carmichaels, Linda asks," didn't you tell them what happened?" Teresa replies," yes I did." Linda asks once again," and this is what they told you to do, go back to fagot." Once again Teresa replied," yes they did." Linda thought to her self this is stupid. If a guy hit me two things would happen. One he's a dead man, two he's on his own, and iam gone.

Chapter 13
SECOND CHANCE

After a few days later, things seems a little better around the house. Linda pretty much done the same routine around the house, the cleaning, the caring for her brothers, and most of all raceing the trash out to the garbage truck. Then one day out playing kick ball with her brothers in the side yard, James kicked the ball next to the neighbor's fence. It was Linda's trun to get the ball. As Linda bent over to pick up the ball, Linda noticed a shadow next to her. When Linda rose up to see who it was, she saw a wild hair, beardy lookin man lookin back at her with a half cocked smile. Linda truned and ran back to her brothers, pointing and laughing at the funny looking man.

When Linda told her brothers what she saw, they too pointed and laughed at the funny looking man. Feeling embarest, the strange man walked away from his clothes line. After the strange man walked away, Linda and her brothers continued to play ball. What Linda didn't know was the strange man was still watching her.

A few days later, Linda has forgotten about the strange man. Untill, Robert hired him to cut the grass. Linda was in the kitchen when she first noticed him in the yard. This time the strange man had a neat cut beard and his hair wasn't quiet as wild. He looked at Linda and gave her another smile through the door way. He just glared at Linda with those baby blue eyes. Linda didn't know what to say. Linda just gave a akward smile back at him and left the kitchen.

As a lawn mower cranked up, Linda came to the window. Linda wanted to see if the stranger was still out there cutting the grass. Yep, he's still out there, Linda thought. Linda decieded to watch him for awhile, mainly to see what he'll do next. Awhile later, the stranger turned off the mower to pull the weeds under the orange tree. Linda noticed how hot it was that day, and how he was wiping his brow to keep the sweat out of his eyes. Linda whent back into the kitchen to fix the strange man a tall glass of ice tea.

When Linda took the glass of ice tea to the door way of the kitchen, the strange man was standing under the orange tree straching his back and legs. Linda called the for the stranger to come over to the door. The stranger came to the door steps and said," yes mam." Linda told the stranger," here is a glass of ice sweet tea." The stranger said," thanks I needed that," as he took the glass. Linda stood there untill the glass was handed back to her. Then Linda just politely smiled at the stranger as she went to put up the glass in the kitchen sink. Linda the scurried to her room and shut the door behind her.

After wahile, it got really quite. Linda wanted to see if the stranger was still out there. Linda just stepped out side to look around for any sign for the stranger. Scences he wasn't in the yard, Linda took a couple steps out on the steps, and laid out on the steps. Linda loved to try to sun bathe, she likes to she how long it would take her to get sick from the sun.

As night came near, Linda's brothers finally made it in the door way. Ofcourse, like always Linda had to make sure her brothers were feed, bathed,and tooken care of for school the next day. When the next day did come around, Linda even tried to get her brothers help with the trash. Eventhought, Linda always took the trash out all by her self.

After sending her brothers off to school, Linda then didn't have anyone to worry about but her self. When Linda got dreesed, she was on her way to the buss stop to catch the buss to school. On her way to the buss stop, a green car just ran right by her going way to fast. The only words that came to her that flew out of her mouth was," *SLOW DOWN STUPID!*" As the car went by Linda, Linda just shook her head from side to side thinking, that idiot is gonna hit someone one day. As she watched the car go by, Linda watched for the tail lights light up but they didn't.

As Linda went to school, Linda thought, at least here there's no reason to worry as much and the kids just stay out of my way. When the bell rings, Linda trys to make her way to her first class. Up the flight of stairs Linda gose, trying not to trip over her feet. Linda just made her seat when the teacher begun to make her roll call. When

Linda's name was called, Linda made a big hearty fart before she could even answer. Linda just couldn't hold it in any more. The kids bursted out laughfing as if it was the most funniest thing they ever heard. Then again the other kids just gasped for air or started to cry for air.

As the teacher came near Linda, she quickly truned away, and opened a window. The teacher then said," Linda next time you feel the need to do that just go ahead and step out of the class, and when you come back and just let me know ok. Linda replied," yes mam." The teacher added," I don't mean to be mean but dang girl that smelled as if something crawled up you and died." Once again the class cracked up with laughter, and left Linda feeling embarrased.

As the class tries to continue with the roll call, Linda had a flash back of when she was in the fith grade. In that class the teacher had to leave the class room to talk with another adult. When she left, a student then reached over to Linda's desk. When doing so, Linda jumped up out of her seat and whent over to were the boy was and demanded her papers back, the boy refused to do so. When the boy refuse to give Linda back her papers, Linda told him," *if you don't give me back my papers, iam gonna blow you away!*" The boy looked at Linda as if she was stupid, while the other kids looked at Linda as if she had a gun. When the boy still refuse to give Linda back her papers, Linda just truned her self around in front of him, and let out the most stinking fart that she could. Then in between gasps of air, the boy gave back Linda's papers. When Linda sat back down at her desk, she told the boy,"

I told you idiot." Just in time for the teacher to come back in the class to say," <u>wow,</u> what died in here?"

Then the bell rang which nocked Linda out of her day dream. As the teacher tried to speak up loader then the bell, the teacher tried to tell her students thire home work asignedments. Linda not listening, just scurried as fast as she could to her next class knowing it would be way on the other side of campas. She finally arrived at the class room door, when bell just rung. When Linda opened the door, a smart mouth student blurted out, *"your late."* This agravaed Linda into saying, *"hay, you'll be late to. If your classes seems to be half mile apart too, every single freakin day."*

All Linda's other classes whent about normal, you go in the class, do your work till the bell rings, then repeat. After school was finally over for the day, Linda cault the buss home. After getting home, Linda wanted to begin her daily chores. Linda thought to her self, were's the mop? Then she saw the mop by the kitchen door. As Linda went to reach for the mop, Linda's brother's brust the the kitchen door open, almost taking her hand with it.

As the boys came runing in the door, they was mumbleing how a green car almost ran them down. Linda told her brothers," next ime stay on the sidewalk." Bobby replied," but sis the sidewalk ends only so far." Linda answers," well then stay near or in the ditch line ok." The boys answers at the same time," yes mam."

Linda reminded her brothers," if ya'll have any home work, then ya'll needed to be doing it." After checking all the home work, to be sure it's done, Linda sent each brother to the bath room to take a bath for tomarrow school day. After thier baths, Linda tried to find some thing for them to put in thier stomakes befor putting to bed. Many times Linda thought how this is suposed to be her mothers job, and how Linda wounders were in Wahneta could be here mother.

By the time Linda has the house straightin up, Teresa and Robert wounders into the house. Teresa asks," Linda did you do the house for me while I was out?" Linda replied," yes mam, I did." Teresa also asks," did you do your home work yet?" Linda also replies," no mam, I didn't have time yet. After cleaning after my brothers, and taking care of them." Robert spoke up saying," bullshit, you had plenty of time. I bet, all you did was watch that dam t.v. all day." Linda responded," *hay, no one is talking to you fagot. Wait till I raddle your chain.*" Irraitated Robert said," *you can't talk to me like that. If you talk to me like that once more, iam gonna stick a pincle in your ear.*" Linda told Robert, "*yea, go ahead, and you'll be a dead man by morning with that pincle stuck up your rear end, scence you like it that way, fagot.*"

Teresa told Linda to shut the hell up and to go to her room. Linda did as she was told, but Linda also cracked the door so she could hear what was being said. Robert told Teresa," you need to go in there and have a talk with her." Teresa replies," yes Junior I know." When Linda heared this she quickly shut the door and sat on her bed. A few seconds later, Teresa walked into Linda's bed room. Befor Teresa could say anything, Linda said," I know you'll gonna take his side you always do. I just wish I could find somebody to love me for me, and not what I could offer him or what he could take from me." Teresa didn't say anything, infact Teresa just droped her head, and left the room. Linda just sat on her bed and cried over her day, and pried to god to take her home or give her another life to live.

After a couple days gone by, everythings seems to be back to normal. Until Linda got home from school. As Linda walked up the drive way Linda saw Robert and Teresa talking to the neigbors at the fence. Linda thought it was a little fishy, but then again she just dismissed it just as easy.

After doing all of the daily chores Linda saw her mother coming in the door with a smile across her face. Linda was a little curious at first, but that died when Teresa said," Linda there's a boy that likes you, and he wants to go out with you." Linda quickly replies," NO WAY! I don't want to go out with any body right now." Just as Linda had finished her sentence, Robert brust into the room saying," Teresa, the boy is coming over right now." Linda tried to get a word in, but couldn't. Teresa and Robert was to excited to listen to what Linda had to say.

When Teresa and Robert whent out side to greet the boy, Linda dashed to her room. After Teresa and Robert retruned to the living room, they saw that Linda wasn't in the living room. Teresa told Junior," tell the boy to wait a minute and i'll get Linda out here. As Robert went out side, Teresa went into Linda's room.

While in the room, Teresa begged Linda to come out and at least meet the boy. Linda after awhile said sarcasticly," fine already, I'll meet him but I don't have to date him right." Teresa replies with a smile," right Linda." As Teresa and Linda walked out of the bed room, they saw that the boy wasn't there. Linda was releaved that the boy wasn't there, eventhough her mother wasn't. Teresa asks," Junior were is he?" Junior told Teresa," he is right out side the door." Teresa said," well, tell him to come in here dummy." Junior gave Teresa a look and went to get the boy.

Waiting to see what happens next, Linda sat on the lounge chair. When the boy came in he sat on the other side of the room. The first thing Linda noticed about him as he sat down was this was no boy, this is a man. Linda started to ask questions about this man claiming to be a boy. The frist question Linda asked was," how old are you?" The man replies," I am 21 years old." Linda begun to add the differnts in thier ages. Linda thought, well I am 13 and that would make it eight years differnts. Well at least were still in the same decade, and besides that in ten days i'll be 14 years old.

Linda the asks," what is your name?" The young man answers," Danny Joe Le'May. As Linda dazed into his baby bule eyes, Linda then realized that he was the one that cut Robert's grass awhile back. After awhile Danny asks," well, do you want to go on a date with me tonight?" Linda thought for a minute as she looked around for an excuse. Secncse Linda couldn't find an excuse not to go, she just said," o.k. why not, it seems as if everything here is done anyway." Danny said," great then i'll pick you up around eight." Linda looked at the clock and said," sure why not o.k. then. I'll see you then. Danny and Linda shook hands as if just made a pack.

Danny left the house with a smile on his face. When he got home his parent asked him why was he is smilein as if he was a yellow cat that swallowed a canery. Danny replies," I have a date tonight. Danny's father replies," remember son you have a curfew." Danny replies," I know, I know dad. I have to be home at 11 o clock. Danny's mother said," that's right son and don't forget it ethier. Danny replies," yes mam."

Mean while back at Robert's house, Robert and Teresa scurried back in the house asking," what happen? Did ya'll get along or what?" Linda calmly answered thier quetions one by one," yes we did get along and yes were going on a date tonight ok." Teresa and Robert looked at each other asif they were very pleased.

Will this mean happyness for Linda or aguish and pure sadness. Find out in the next book.

THE END OR MAYBE NOT YOUR CALL